Our Favorite Pets

Crazy About Puppies

Harold Morris

TABLE OF CONTENTS

- Puppies 2
- Glossary 22
- Index 23

A Crabtree Seedlings Book

Puppies

Baby animals are cute!

Some baby animals, such as baby dogs, make great **pets**.

Baby dogs are called puppies.

litter (LIT-ur)

Some mother dogs may have just one puppy at a time. Others may have many.

PUPPY FACTS!

When a mother dog has a group of puppies born at the same time, it is called a **litter** of puppies.

A puppy often looks like its mother.

The mother dog takes care of the puppies. She licks them to keep them clean.

Newborn puppies drink milk from their mother. This helps them grow.

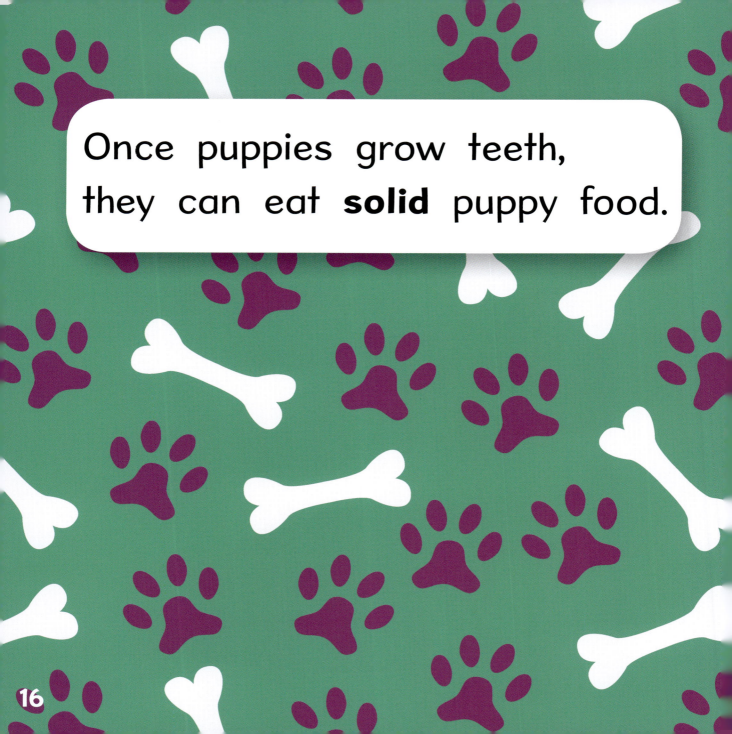

Once puppies grow teeth, they can eat **solid** puppy food.

Puppies have baby teeth. When their teeth fall out, **adult** teeth grow in their place.

Dogs and puppies like to chew things.

PUPPY FACTS!
Chewing dog **treats** helps keep a dog's teeth clean.

Puppies love to play.
They love to sleep too!

Glossary

adult (uh-DUHLT): An adult is a fully grown person or animal.

litter (LIT-ur): A litter is a group of puppies born to the same mother at the same time.

newborn (NOO-born): A newborn is recently born.

pets (PETS): Pets are animals that people keep and take care of for pleasure.

solid (SOL-id): A solid is hard and firm, not runny like a liquid.

treats (TREETS): Dog treats are made for dogs. Treats are usually given to reward good behavior, or to help clean the dog's teeth.

Index

food   16
milk   15
pets   5
teeth   16, 19, 20
treats   20

School-to-Home Support for Caregivers and Teachers

This book helps children grow by letting them practice reading. Here are a few guiding questions to help the reader build his or her comprehension skills. Possible answers appear here in red.

Before Reading
- **What do I think this book is about?** I think this book is about the funny things that puppies do. I think this book is about how to play with puppies.
- **What do I want to learn about this topic?** I want to learn more about taking care of puppies. I want to learn how old a puppy should be to leave its mother.

During Reading
- **I wonder why...** I wonder why puppies make great pets. I wonder why some dogs have only one puppy while other dogs have many puppies.
- **What have I learned so far?** I have learned that when a mother dog has a group of puppies born at the same time, we call it a litter of puppies. I have learned that a puppy often looks like its mother.

After Reading
- **What details did I learn about this topic?** I have learned that the mother dog licks the puppies to keep them clean. I have learned that puppies have baby teeth that fall out and that adult teeth grow in their place.
- **Read the book again and look for the glossary words.** I see the word *litter* on page 9, and the word *treats* on page 20. The other glossary words are found on pages 22 and 23.

Library and Archives Canada Cataloguing in Publication

CIP available at Library and Archives Canada

Library of Congress Cataloging-in-Publication Data

CIP available at Library of Congress

Crabtree Publishing Company
www.crabtreebooks.com   1–800–387–7650

Print book version produced jointly with Blue Door Education in 2022

Written by: Harold Morris
Print coordinator: Katherine Berti

Printed in the U.S.A./CG20210915/012022

Content produced and published by Blue Door Education, Melbourne Beach FL USA. This title Copyright Blue Door Education. All rights reserved. No part of this book may be reproduced or utilized in any form or by any means, electronic or mechanical including photocopying, recording, or by any information storage and retrieval system without permission in writing from the publisher.

PHOTO CREDITS:
Cover photo © Sonsedska Yuliia; background illustration on cover and throughout book © Kannaa; Page 3 © Voren1; Page 4 © ulkas; Page 5 © IRYNA KAZLOVA; Page 7 © Ksenia Merenkova; Page 8 © Eric Isselee; Page 9 © artush; Page 10 © Eric Issele; Page 11 © Nejron Photo (bottom), © cynoclub (top); Page 13 © framsook; Page 14 © Revaphoto; Page 15 © MirasWonderland; Page 17 © Africa Studio; Page 18 © exies; Page 19 © 1stGallery; Page 20 © Chalabala; Page 21 © Smitt; Page 22 © Ljupco, © Artush, © Toloubaev, © anurakpong; Page 23 © Africa Studio, © Chalabala All photos from Shutterstock.com and Istockphoto.com

Published in the United States
Crabtree Publishing
347 Fifth Ave.
Suite 1402-145
New York, NY 10016

Published in Canada
Crabtree Publishing
616 Welland Ave.
St. Catharines, Ontario
L2M 5V6